Autumn
Publishing

Down in the deepest ocean, there once lived a mermaid princess called Ariel. She was the youngest daughter of King Triton, ruler of the merpeople, and she had the most beautiful singing voice in the whole of his kingdom.

Her father loved her dearly, but she was always getting into trouble. Ariel longed to be part of the human world and spent her time exploring old shipwrecks.

When Ariel was sixteen years old, King Triton arranged for her to sing in a magnificent concert, and merpeople came from all over the kingdom to hear her.

That evening, however, Ariel was so busy exploring with her friend Flounder that she forgot all about the concert!

She had found some human treasures and taken them to the surface to ask Scuttle the seagull what they were.

The Sea-King feared for her safety and, thinking humans were dangerous, warned her to stay away from them. But the little mermaid was certain he was wrong.

King Triton was furious. "You could have been seen by one of those humans!" he raged. "I'm never to hear of you going to the surface again. Is that clear?"

Ariel tried to protest, but her father wouldn't listen.

King Triton ordered Sebastian, Ariel's music teacher, to keep an eye on her. But it wasn't an easy task!

One day, Sebastian followed Ariel and Flounder to the surface to watch a ship.

On board, the crew were celebrating the birthday of a handsome prince called Eric, and Ariel watched them in delight.

Soon, storm clouds gathered overhead. Huge waves wrecked the ship and Eric was flung into the sea. Ariel swam quickly to his rescue and pulled him towards the shore.

"Look! He's breathing!" cried Ariel. She gazed at Eric and fell deeply in love. Then, as she sang to him, his eyes began to open. But, hearing a voice in the distance, Ariel slipped back into the water and hid behind a nearby rock. She watched as Eric's servant led him away.

When they were out of sight, Ariel swam home.
"Some day," she vowed to herself, "I'm going to be part of
that human world."

Sebastian had seen everything and it was not long before
the Sea-King learnt that Ariel was in love with a human.

King Triton was very angry. Determined to teach his
daughter a lesson, he stormed into her secret grotto and
destroyed all her beloved human treasures.

Ariel was heartbroken. Then, two sly-looking eels called Flotsam and Jetsam appeared.

"We know someone who can make all your dreams come true," they hissed. "Ursula has great powers."

"The Sea-Witch!" gasped Ariel. She knew that Ursula was her father's worst enemy. Ursula had been banished from the kingdom many years ago and was now seeking revenge.

Ariel hesitated. Then, thinking that it was her only chance to win Prince Eric's love, the little mermaid swam away with the evil eels.

Ursula greeted Ariel gleefully. "The only way to get what you want," the Sea-Witch explained, "is to become human yourself. And fortunately I know a little magic."

"Now listen, here's the deal. In exchange for your voice, I will turn you into a human for three days. If Eric hasn't given you the kiss of true love in that time, you will become a mermaid again and belong to me forever."

A scroll appeared in Ursula's hand. "Go ahead and sign," she urged. Ariel was terrified, but, thinking of Eric again, she signed. A moment later she was walking on the seashore – a human at last.

Prince Eric had been searching everywhere for the girl with the beautiful voice who had rescued him. He had almost given up hope of finding her, when he noticed someone sitting on a rock.

This girl looked familiar, but when he found she couldn't speak, Eric realised sadly that she wasn't the one.

Feeling sorry for the voiceless girl, he led her back to the palace. And the next day, Eric took Ariel on a tour of his kingdom. They enjoyed being together and Ariel was sure the prince was falling in love with her.

Later that afternoon, when they were boating on a lake, Eric bent forwards to kiss Ariel – but at that very moment, the boat was overturned.

The Sea-Witch had been watching them and fearing her plan was about to fail, she sent her precious eels to take action.

Later, Ursula disguised herself as a beautiful maiden named Vanessa and wore a seashell necklace containing Ariel's voice.

She made her way to the shore, where she captured Prince Eric under her spell.

Eric led Vanessa to the palace and the very next day announced that they were to be married. The wedding ship was to depart at sunset.

Ariel and her friends watched in despair as the sun lowered in the sky.

By chance, Scuttle discovered that Vanessa was really Ursula in disguise and he called on all the sea creatures to stop the wedding. Sebastian went to find the Sea-King and Flounder helped Ariel towards the wedding ship.

Suddenly, birds swooped down on Vanessa. A lobster pinched her nose and some seals flipped her into the wedding cake!

In the chaos, Vanessa's seashell necklace broke and the beautiful voice inside flew back to its rightful owner.

Eric, released from the spell, took Ariel in his arms.
Just as he was about to kiss her, the sun sank below
the horizon. Straightaway, Ariel was turned back into
a mermaid.

Ursula grabbed her and dived into the water. Her evil
cackle echoed eerily around the ship.

"Ursula, stop!" thundered King Triton, rearing up
in front of the Sea-Witch. "Let her go!"

"No!" cried Ursula. "She's mine now. You see, we made a deal! However, I might be willing to make an exchange for someone even better," she suggested, slyly.

King Triton felt he had no choice. He changed the signature on the scroll to his own and handed over his magic trident to the Sea-Witch.

"At last! It's all mine," Ursula screamed. "I am the ruler of the ocean!" Just then, a sharp pain shot through her arm. It was a harpoon thrown by Eric. He had come to rescue Ariel.

The Sea-Witch swelled with anger and towered above them. She summoned all the sea's power and stirred up a giant whirlpool, dragging up ancient shipwrecks from the seabed.

Eric scrambled on board one of the decks and,
somehow, he reached the ship's steering wheel. Using all
his might, he aimed the broken bow directly at Ursula.

And with a terrible scream, the evil Sea-Witch
disappeared under the sea.

King Triton's power was instantly restored. He rose to the surface and saw Ariel gazing lovingly at Eric, who was lying on the beach.

"She really does love him," Triton murmured to Sebastian. "I suppose the only problem left is how much I will miss her."

Then, with a flourish of his trident, the Sea-King granted Ariel her dearest wish – to be human forever. Overjoyed, Eric and Ariel rushed into each other's arms.

A few days later, the couple were married and all their friends were invited to the wedding. King Triton gladly gave Ariel and Eric his blessing, knowing they would live happily ever after.